GLEN ROCK PUBLIC LIBRARY
315 ROCK ROAD
GLEN ROCK, N.J. 07452

POINTERS

TRUCKS

Written by Andrew Salter
Illustrated by Ian Moores, Mike Saunders, and Gerald Witcomb

RAINTREE
STECK-VAUGHN
PUBLISHERS
The Steck-Vaughn Company

Austin, Texas

© Copyright 1995, Steck-Vaughn Company

All rights reserved. No part of this book may be reproduced or utilized in any form or by any means, electronic or mechanical, including photocopying, recording, or by any information storage and retrieval system, without permission in writing from the Publisher. Inquiries should be addressed to: Copyright Permissions, Steck-Vaughn Company, P.O. Box 26015, Austin, TX 78755

Editor: Frank Tarsitano
Project Manager: Julie Klaus

Library of Congress Cataloging-in-Publication Data
Salter, Andrew, 1969–
    Trucks / written by Andrew Salter; illustrated by Ian Moores, Mike Saunders, and Gerald Witcomb.
      p.   cm. — (Pointers)
    Includes index.
    ISBN 0-8114-6189-0
    1. Trucks — Juvenile literature. [1. Trucks.] I. Moores, Ian, Ill.
II. Saunders, Mike, ill. III. Witcomb, Gerald, ill. IV. Title. V. Series.
TL230.15.S25 1995
629.224—dc20   93-49568
                                                        CIP
                                                        AC

Printed and bound in the United States

1 2 3 4 5 6 7 8 9 0 VH 99 98 97 96 95 94

Foreword

This book is about different types of trucks and the jobs they are designed to do. It includes information about huge delivery trucks, gasoline tankers, car carriers, the big dump trucks you see on construction sites, and even racing trucks.

Nearly everything we buy today has been carried on the roads by trucks. The size of these trucks varies from country to country. Some trucks in Europe carry up to 44 tons, while tonnage limits in the United States vary from state to state. The power of truck engines is measured in horsepower (hp). Most countries have laws limiting how fast trucks can be driven.

Truck drivers are highly trained. Not only do they have to pass a strict driving test, but they also have to take written exams if they carry hazardous materials. To carry certain types of hazardous loads, an operator needs a special license. Trucks are built to very high safety standards to protect the public and the driver. Some trucks have lots of gears—often as many as 18. Some have automatic or semi-automatic transmissions.

Most trucks are powered by diesel engines, but because of air pollution, manufacturers are designing their engines to be cleaner. In the future we may see trucks running on new kinds of fuels.

Contents

6 Straight Truck

8 Concrete Mixer

10 End Dump Truck

12 Drawbar Truck

14 Refrigerated Truck

16 Conventional Tractor

18 Car Carrier

20 Dump Truck

22 Racing Truck

24 Garbage Truck

26 Tank Truck

28 Low Boy

30 Glossary

32 Index

▶ Straight Truck

The Volvo FS7 is a modern medium-sized straight truck. With a powerful engine and ruggedly built body, it can carry loads of up to 17 tons—its gross vehicle weight.

Trucks that do not tow a trailer behind them are called straight trucks. A truck with two axles is called a 4x2, which tells you it has four wheels and that two of them are drive wheels. This truck has four wheels attached to the drive axle.

Volvo produces the FS7 as a unit made up of the chassis, engine, and cab. This is called a chassis-cab. Customers can choose what type of body they want attached to the chassis-cab.

4 The basic body frame, or chassis, is made from high-strength steel. Different types of truck bodies can also be attached to the chassis.

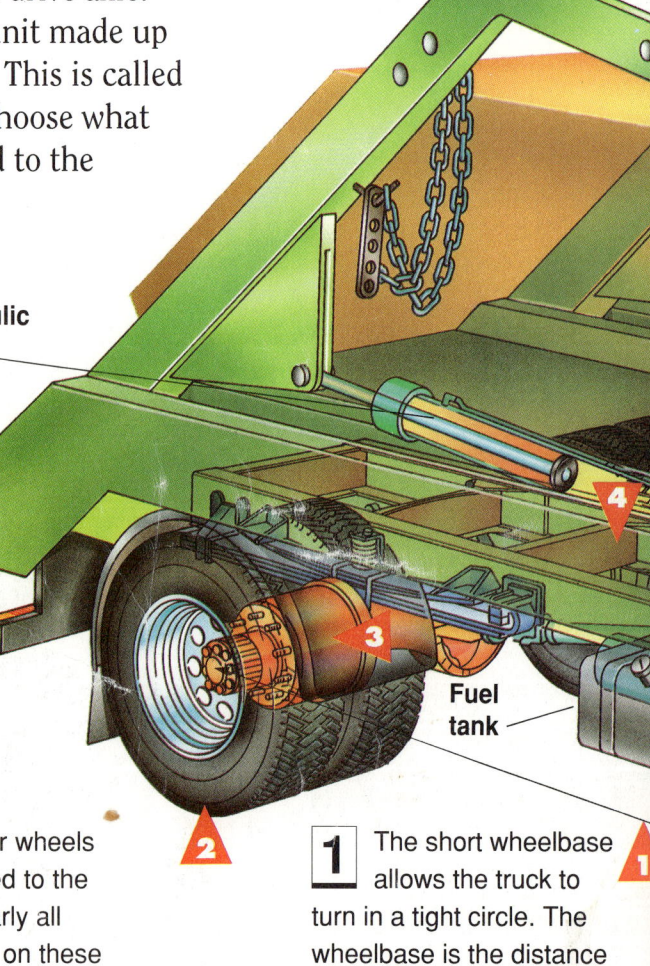

Hydraulic ram

3 Large wheels, much bigger than those on cars, carry the weight of the truck body. The rear axle is the drive axle. It gets its power from the engine through the transmission. The front axle is the steering axle.

Fuel tank

2 Double rear wheels are attached to the drive axle of nearly all trucks. The tires on these wheels give a better grip and spread a load's weight.

1 The short wheelbase allows the truck to turn in a tight circle. The wheelbase is the distance between the front and rear axle.

5 This truck has a manual eight-speed synchromesh transmission, with low crawler and reverse gears. An automatic transmission could be provided if desired.

6 The small seven-liter turbocharged engine has six cylinders and can produce 230 hp.

▲ *The hydraulic-powered arms of the cargo-loader lift the cargo up using chains. They swing the cargo onto the truck.*

Protective headboard

Exhaust pipe

Sunroof

Concrete Mixer

This type of six-wheel straight truck is a 6x6—all the axles drive all the wheels. The 6x4 truck is also very popular in the construction industry, particularly for concrete mixers.

This truck can carry a maximum of 26 tons. The mixer itself holds 7.8 cubic yards (6 cu. m) of concrete. The weight is held very high off the ground, so the twin axles are needed in the rear to keep the truck stable.

3 The big steel drum revolves as the truck drives along to the construction site. This keeps the concrete inside the drum from getting hard before the truck arrives at its destination.

2 The mixed concrete is poured out of the chute into wheelbarrows at a construction site. The bottom part of the chute folds away when the truck is on the road.

1 Both axles at the rear of the truck are drive axles. The additional drive axle at the front of the truck can be engaged to give extra grip when the truck is driven off-road.

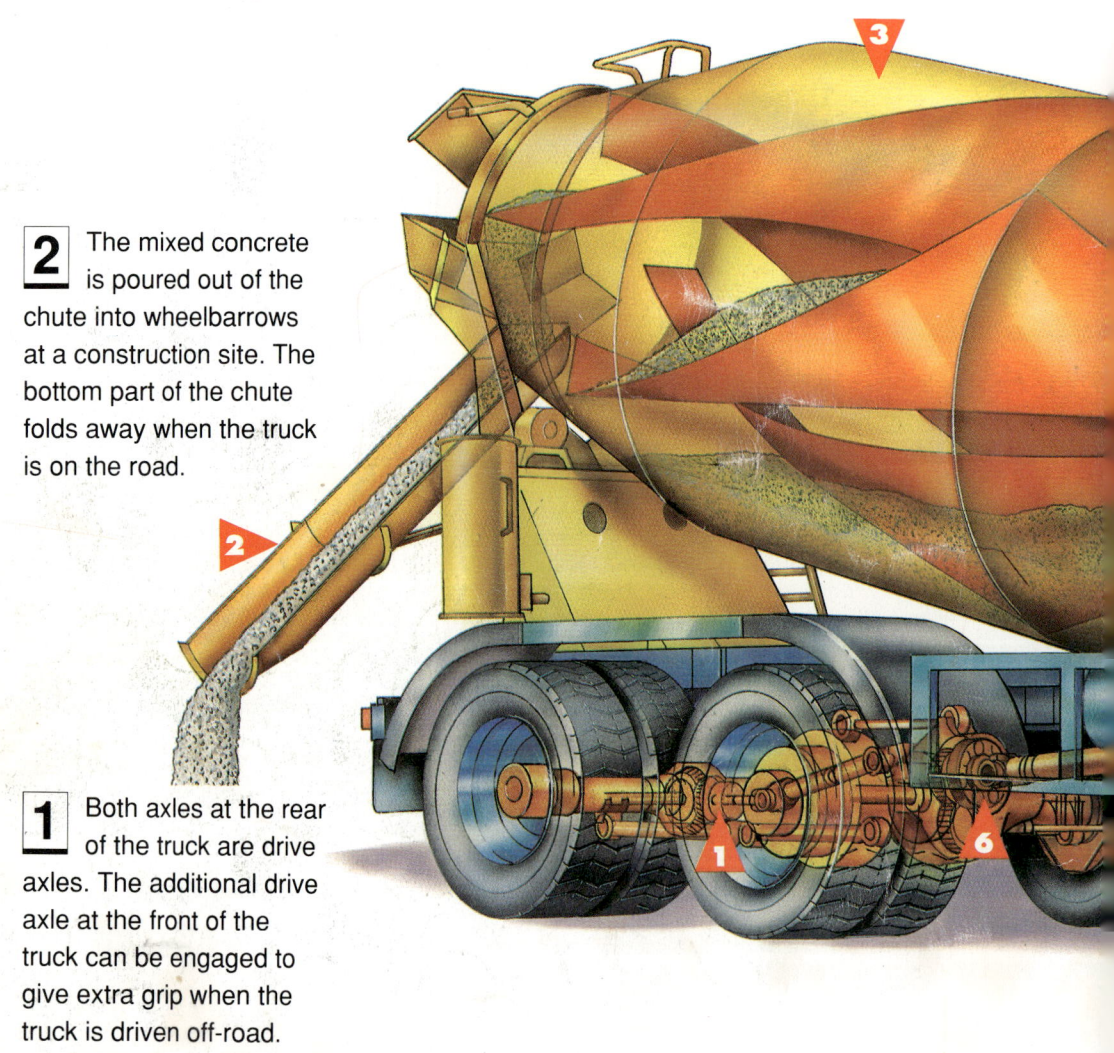

4 A water tank is mounted between the drum and the cab. It holds the water for the driver to wash the mixer out when unloading has finished.

5 The exhaust stack is vertical, so it will not stir up dust when the truck is working at a construction site or quarry.

6 Differential locks can be engaged on the rear axles from a lever in the cab. If the rear wheels start to spin, the axles can be locked together so that they turn together, giving them extra drive.

Sun visor

Engine fan

Gearshift

End Dump Truck

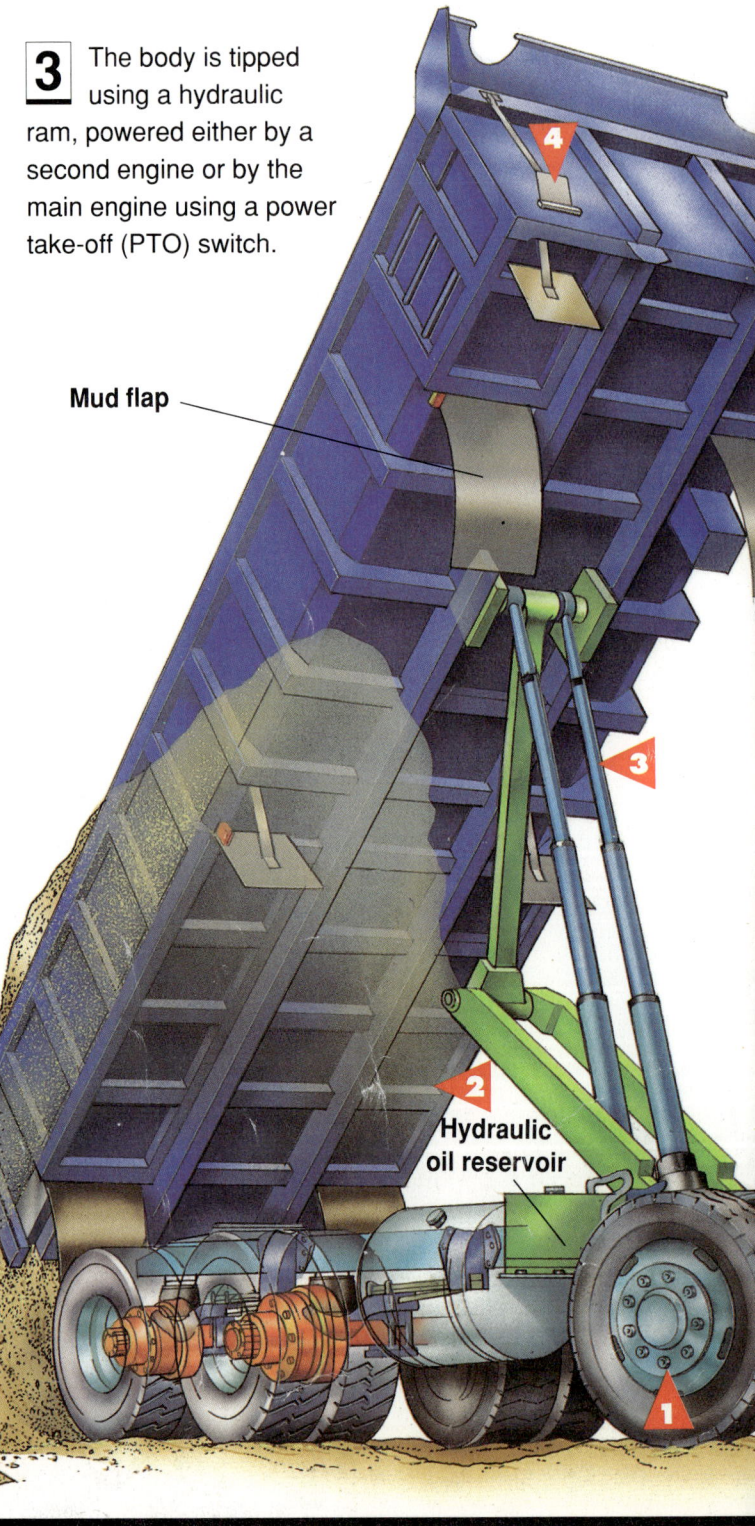

2 Huge loads of materials are often called "bulk" goods. They are carried in the high-sided end dump body, which is usually made of steel. Truckers try to carry as much cargo as possible, so the body may be made of lightweight aluminum, giving a payload of 22 tons of bulk goods.

3 The body is tipped using a hydraulic ram, powered either by a second engine or by the main engine using a power take-off (PTO) switch.

Mud flap

1 The extra axle on the front of this truck is a steering axle. As well as allowing extra weight to be carried, it helps the truck remain stable, especially when going around corners.

Hydraulic oil reservoir

End dump trucks deliver the huge loads of materials used in house and road building. They also carry large loads of farm products, such as grain and sugar beets.

This eight-wheeler end dump has four axles. The back two power the truck while the front two steer. Because of the extra axle, it can carry six more tons than a six-wheeler. The weight is spread out, causing less damage to the surface of the road.

The truck here is a Foden 4350. The 4 stands for 4000 series model; the 350 means it has a 350 hp engine. Since 1981, Foden has been owned by the American manufacturer Paccar.

4 Most end dump drivers carry a shovel. If the load is wet, it may not come out of the body easily, so the driver will have to climb into the body to scrape out the corners of the truck.

Air intake

Horns

5 The front grille can be lifted up so that daily checks can be made on water and oil levels.

6 The chassis is built high off the ground so that the bottom of the truck is not damaged by large boulders when working in quarries or on farms with rocky ground.

Drawbar Truck

A drawbar truck is a combination straight truck and a trailer pulled behind it. A full trailer has two sets of wheels—one set in front and one in back. A semitrailer has only a rear set of wheels. The straight truck is like the one on page 6. The trailer and straight truck are locked together by a coupling at the back of the truck.

Most states restrict the length of trucks, the maximum weight carried on one axle, and how many trailers may be attached. In some states up to three trailers are permitted. The length of the drawbar combination is about 60 feet (18 m). Some drawbar trailers have dual wheels in the middle; this one has an axle and turntable connector at the front for stability.

1 Side rails are built along the truck and trailer to prevent people from getting caught under the wheels. With a truck of this length this could happen without the driver noticing.

2 Legs that drop down and can support the box body allow the truck and trailer to pull out from underneath. The truck itself can then be used for something else.

3 The body is where the cargo is stored. This body can be detached and can stand on legs.

4 Flexible side panels made of a very strong material are unclipped and drawn open to load the vehicle. The curtains are then closed, and the truck is ready to go.

▼ *The trailer is steered by its front axle, which swivels around on a turntable. This makes the drawbar easier to maneuver despite its length.*

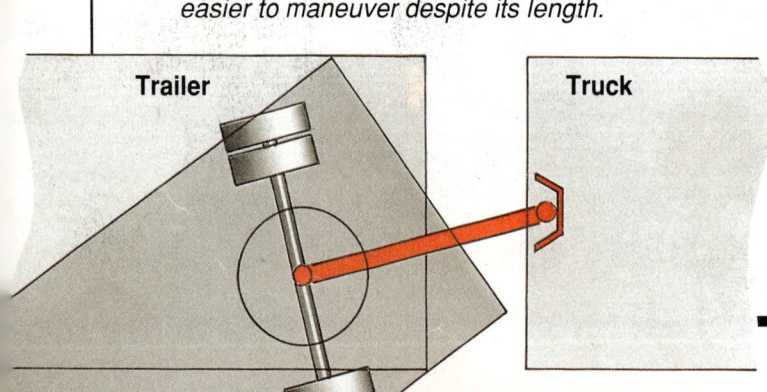

Trailer / Truck

Panel straps

5 Some trucks have sleeper compartments. Truck drivers are likely to be away from home for days at a time, and most have to sleep in the cab. The driver climbs up a ladder into the berth.

6 The cab is where the driver sits. It is built on top of the engine, giving the driver a very good view of the road. Driving a drawbar truck in reverse gear is very difficult, so large mirrors are placed on the side of the car to help the driver see where he or she is going.

Hatch to sleeper compartment

13

▶ Refrigerated Truck

3 A thermometer is mounted outside the trailer. Once a cargo is loaded, the doors are not opened again until the truck is unloaded. The truck driver checks the thermometer to make sure the temperature inside stays the same.

Insulated box body

2 This semitrailer has three axles and an "air bag" suspension. This gives a much softer ride than the more usual steel suspension. It protects the cargo being carried and causes less damage to the road.

Support leg

1 Wooden pallets hold the cargo before it is loaded into the trailer. The driver has to exchange the loaded pallets for empty ones, which are stored under the trailer out of the way.

This refrigerated truck is a combination of a tractor in front coupled with a tri-axle semitrailer pulled behind. This means the semitrailer has three axles, and its front rests on the tractor. A tractor like this is connected to a semitrailer by a coupling known as a "fifth wheel." The refrigerated trailer is 44.6 feet (13.6 m) long and 13.7 feet (4.2 m) high. It is an insulated box with a refrigeration unit on the front run by a separate motor.

4 The refrigeration unit on the front of the semitrailer works independently of the tractor engine. A cargo can be kept at a constant temperature even if the tractor is not connected.

5 An aerodynamic air deflector saves fuel by cutting down wind resistance. A fully loaded truck like this can travel 12 miles (100 km) on 9 gallons (40 liters) of fuel.

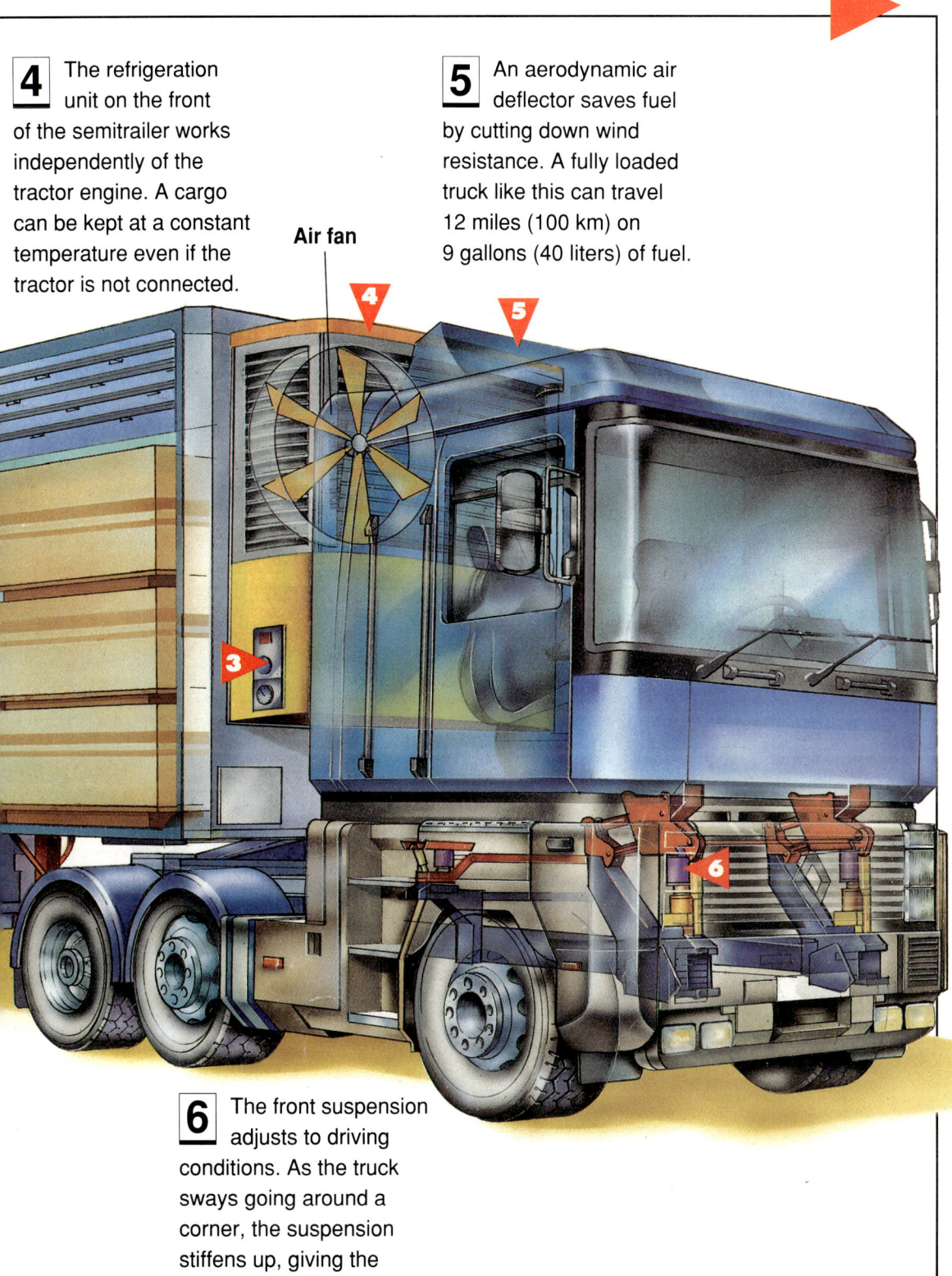

Air fan

6 The front suspension adjusts to driving conditions. As the truck sways going around a corner, the suspension stiffens up, giving the driver a more stable ride.

Conventional Tractor

This Freightliner FLD 112 conventional tractor has a high roof cab, designed for coast-to-coast running across North America. Freightliner custom-makes both conventional tractors with the engine in front of the cab and cab-over tractors with the cab set over the engine.

In the United States overall length restrictions on trucks are different from those in Europe. An operator in the United States can use longer trucks, so the manufacturers can design more freely. The conventional tractor is very distinctive. Aluminum is used in its construction to make the tractor very light in weight. Freightliner is owned by Mercedes and sells thousands of these tractors a year.

Fifth wheel

Mud flap

2 Freightliner trucks are made with a 13-speed transmission. There are 13 forward gears and a reverse gear.

1 Side skirts and air deflectors improve the look of the tractor and fuel efficiency. Truck manufacturers try to make their tractors as streamlined as possible.

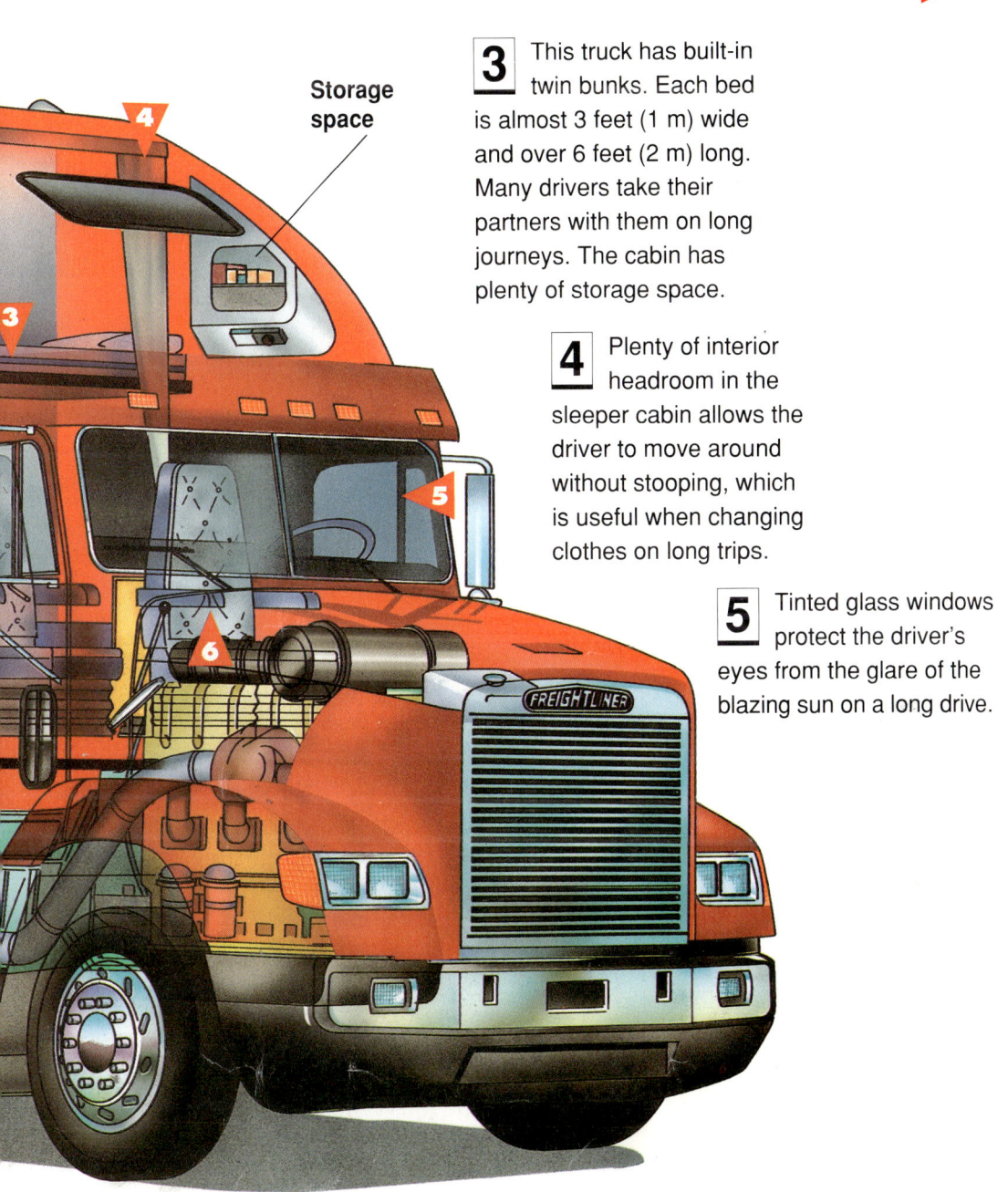

Storage space

3 This truck has built-in twin bunks. Each bed is almost 3 feet (1 m) wide and over 6 feet (2 m) long. Many drivers take their partners with them on long journeys. The cabin has plenty of storage space.

4 Plenty of interior headroom in the sleeper cabin allows the driver to move around without stooping, which is useful when changing clothes on long trips.

5 Tinted glass windows protect the driver's eyes from the glare of the blazing sun on a long drive.

6 Air-suspended seats are built into the tractor to help the driver be more comfortable during the long hours behind the wheel.

▶ Car Carrier

3 The cars are held on the car carrier by a series of stopping bars and straps. Cars can only be attached to the truck at certain points agreed on by the carmakers.

Safety rail

Berth

2 Steps are built into the side of the cab for the driver to climb up. In a cab-over truck the driver sits very high up.

1 Each axle has large drum brakes. When the brake pedal is pressed, air is released into the system. A brake shoe rubs against the drum, slowing the truck down.

4 Loading ramps are lifted up and down, so the cars can be driven onto them. Hydraulic rams that are operated by remote control move the ramps.

This car carrier is a drawbar combination. It has only one connection or articulation point. This is the "fifth wheel" where the truck and trailer are linked.

Before the 1950s, new cars were delivered individually. Once cars became more popular, they needed to be delivered in bulk. Truck trailers were designed that could carry many cars. The Mk V car is one of the few trailers that can carry 12 full-size cars. Driving a car carrier is a very skilled job.

5 The trailer has a low clearance of about 6 inches (15 cm) to make it more stable and reduce the risk of toppling over on a bend. Car carriers are often over 16 feet (5 m) high.

6 Hydraulic rams pull the trailer and tractor together to reduce drag. The gap between them causes problems with aerodynamics. The rams move the two apart for cornering.

Dump Truck

Giant dump trucks are among the toughest, most powerful trucks used anywhere in the world. They carry massive loads, usually in quarries or on construction sites. Their drivers must be highly trained to operate these trucks, which are sometimes over 21 feet (6.45 m) high.

Some dump trucks have electronic traction aid devices. If the drive wheels start to spin, the brakes are applied, and the torque of the engine is transferred to the tires, giving them better traction. Makers of regular on-the-road trucks are starting to build these systems into their trucks.

3 The largest dump trucks have a massive 110 cubic yard (84 cu. m) body and can carry over 180 tons. Enormous hydraulic rams are needed to lift and tip such a heavy load.

2 This truck has a diesel-electric drive system. A massive 12-cylinder, 2,475 hp engine provides power for an electric generator. Two electric motors, one on each rear wheel, drive the dump truck as it hauls its huge loads.

Chassis rail

1 The tires are specifically designed for off-road work because this type of dump truck is not usually allowed on the roads. The tires are made of very hard rubber with a chunky tread to give good grip.

Mirror

4 The front end of the dumper protects the driver who sits very high up—over 20 feet (6 m) up in some vehicles. A large windshield and lots of mirrors give the driver good visibility.

5 Two big air filters clean the air for the engine. A diesel engine needs clean air to operate and without filters would soon clog up in dusty conditions.

Handrail

6 The driver climbs into the cab using the ladder mounted on the side of the truck. Two big chocks stored at the front are used to keep the truck from slipping when it is dumping a load on a hill.

Chock

Racing Truck

▲ A cab-over truck has the engine under the cab. When mechanics need to work on the engine, the cab tilts over on hinges at the front. A pump works two hydraulic rams, which push the cab over. The engine is exposed, so the mechanics have plenty of room to work on it.

3 An antiroll cage in the cab protects the driver in case of an accident, and antiroll bars built into the chassis help keep the truck stable when cornering at high speeds.

Air intake

Racing harne

1 A turbocharged diesel engine with a power rating of over 1,500 hp drives this truck. It is three times more powerful than most trucks.

2 The front headlights are taped up on the racing truck. If a stone flies up, the tape stops the glass from shattering.

Truck racing is organized along the lines of Formula One Grand Prix car racing. Races often attract crowds of 100,000 spectators.

All racing truck engines are finely tuned for maximum performance. Many have automatic transmissions. On the track, racing trucks are usually limited to 100 mph (160 kph) in the interest of safety, but they are capable of speeds up to 150 mph (240 kph).

In standard speed tests some racing trucks have a pickup as fast as some powerful cars. This racing truck is made by Mercedes, which builds many successful racing trucks.

4 The small fuel tank is mounted across the chassis. On regular trucks, it would be on the side of the tractor between the front and rear axles.

5 Side skirts to help streamlining are attached to racing trucks to increase their speed. On road-going trucks, they are attached to save fuel.

6 High-speed tires like the ones used on fire engines are attached to racing trucks. They have the top layer of tread removed to reduce friction.

Exhaust pipe

Garbage Truck

Special trucks are used in many countries to remove the vast quantities of garbage we produce. This is a straight truck, with a Phoenix 15 body with crew cab. It has a 19.6 cubic yard (15 cu. m) body and a wheelbase of 13.4 feet (4.07 m). The hydraulic pump used for crushing garbage, the packing mechanism, works directly off the engine crankshaft. This allows the packing cycle to be operated while the truck is moving and makes a power take-off (PTO) mechanism unnecessary.

3 The spacious crew cab is designed to seat five workers as well as the driver.

2 The driver has an excellent view thanks to the 6-feet- (2-m-) wide windshield and the high driving position. This is important when weaving through narrow streets in towns and cities.

1 Two towing "eyes" are attached to the front of the truck. If the truck gets stuck at a dump site, it can be pulled free by connecting a towrope to these eyes.

4 This garbage truck has big doors almost 6 feet (1.8 m) wide and large side steps. The crew members wear heavy boots and protective overalls and need plenty of room to climb in and out.

▲
The garbage goes in a container which can hold 207 cubic yards (2.1 cu. m) of garbage. The crushing operation, or packing cycle, takes 25 seconds and loading new garbage can begin 7 seconds after the crushing operation begins.

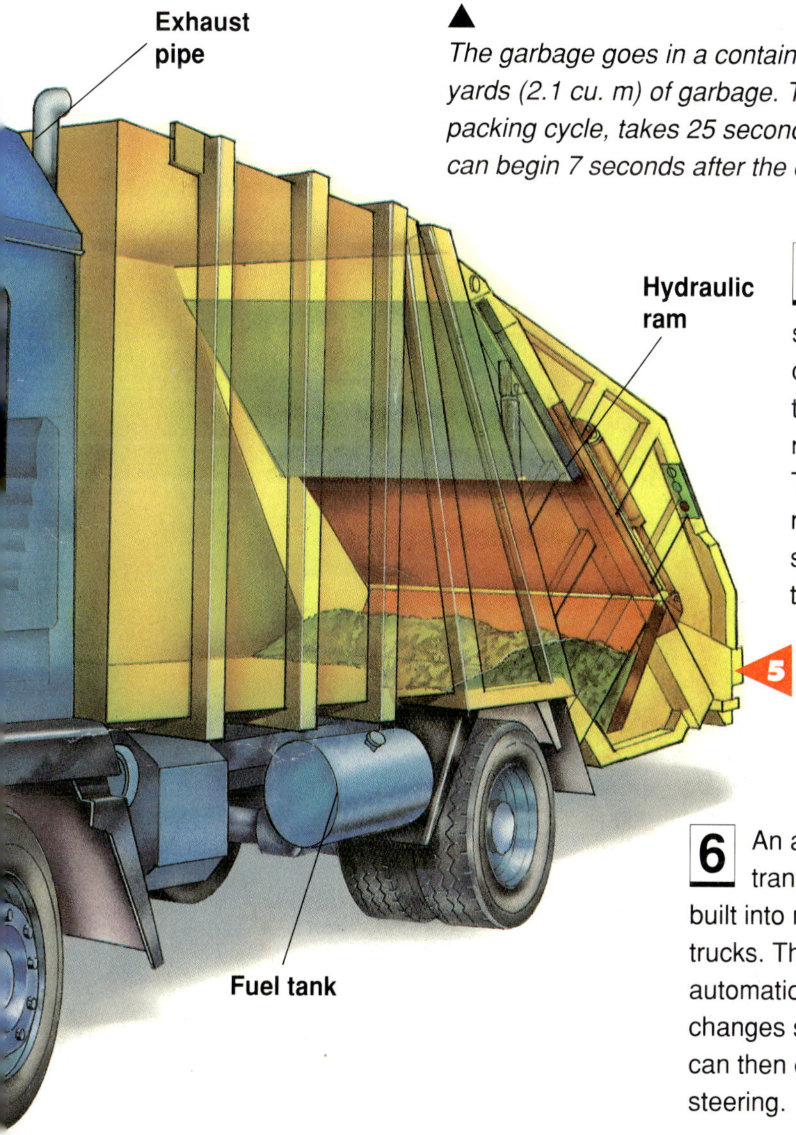

Exhaust pipe

Hydraulic ram

5 The rear panel is activated by a master switch in the cab, but controls at the rear of the truck can start, stop, and reverse the crushing cycle. There is a button at the rear of the truck that sounds a bell to signal the driver to move on.

Fuel tank

6 An automatic transmission is built into many garbage trucks. The gears change automatically as the truck changes speed. The driver can then concentrate on steering.

25

Tank Truck

Tank trucks, or tankers, can carry a huge range of goods, including milk, gasoline, and dangerous chemicals. Tanker drivers must be experts in handling their trucks and also know all about the goods they are carrying. They have to know how to deal with spills, fires, and explosions.

This tractor is an American-built Mack. The law in the United States allows for longer overall truck lengths than in Europe, so tractors are longer. This Mack is a conventional tractor described in more detail on pages 16-17.

3 A tanker that carries liquids is divided into sections to keep the liquids from sloshing around and making driving more difficult.

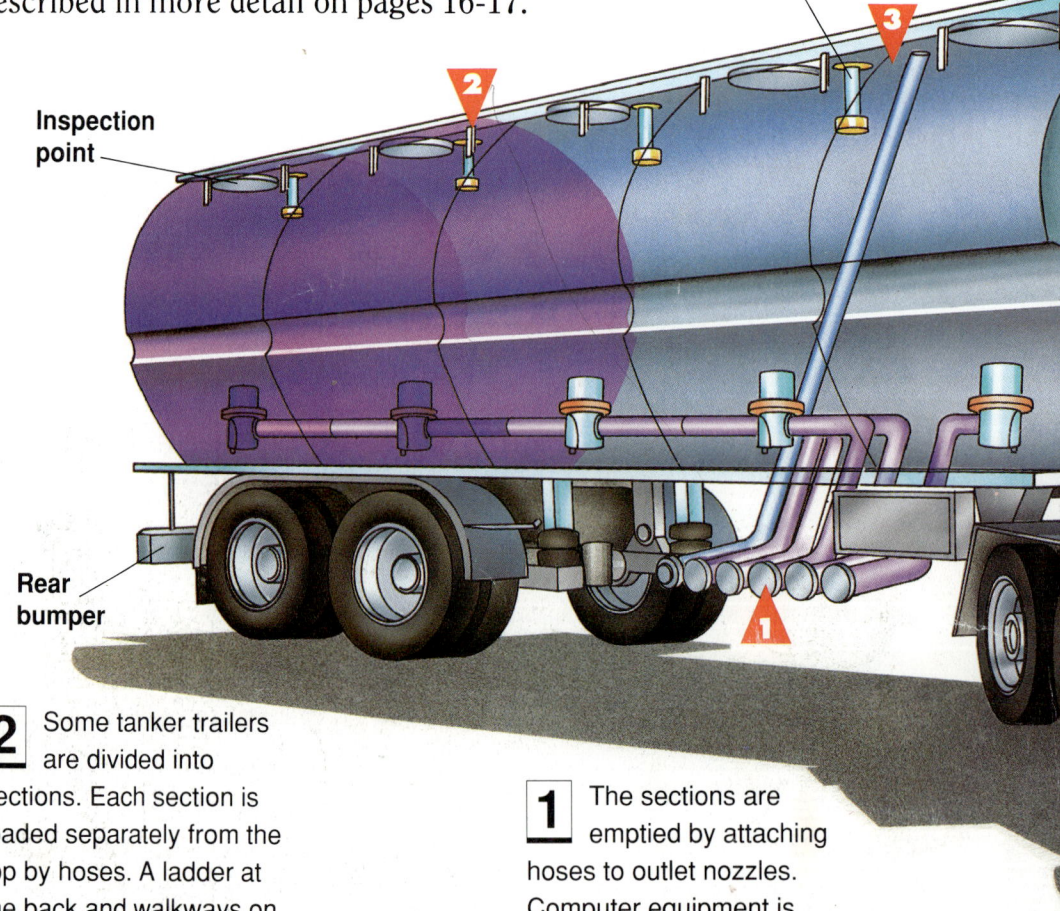

Liquid level indicator

Inspection point

Rear bumper

2 Some tanker trailers are divided into sections. Each section is loaded separately from the top by hoses. A ladder at the back and walkways on the top allow the driver to supervise the work.

1 The sections are emptied by attaching hoses to outlet nozzles. Computer equipment is often used to measure the amount of liquid delivered.

4 Brakes on modern trucks are activated by compressed air at a pressure of 120 pounds per square inch (psi). Twirling hoses connect the trailer to the air and electrical systems of the tractor.

5 A radio antenna sends and receives radio signals. On long-distance trips, a truck driver spends many hours alone and keeps in touch with others by two-way radio.

6 Hazardous cargo signs are placed at the front of the tractor and the rear of the trailer to warn people about the cargo being carried.

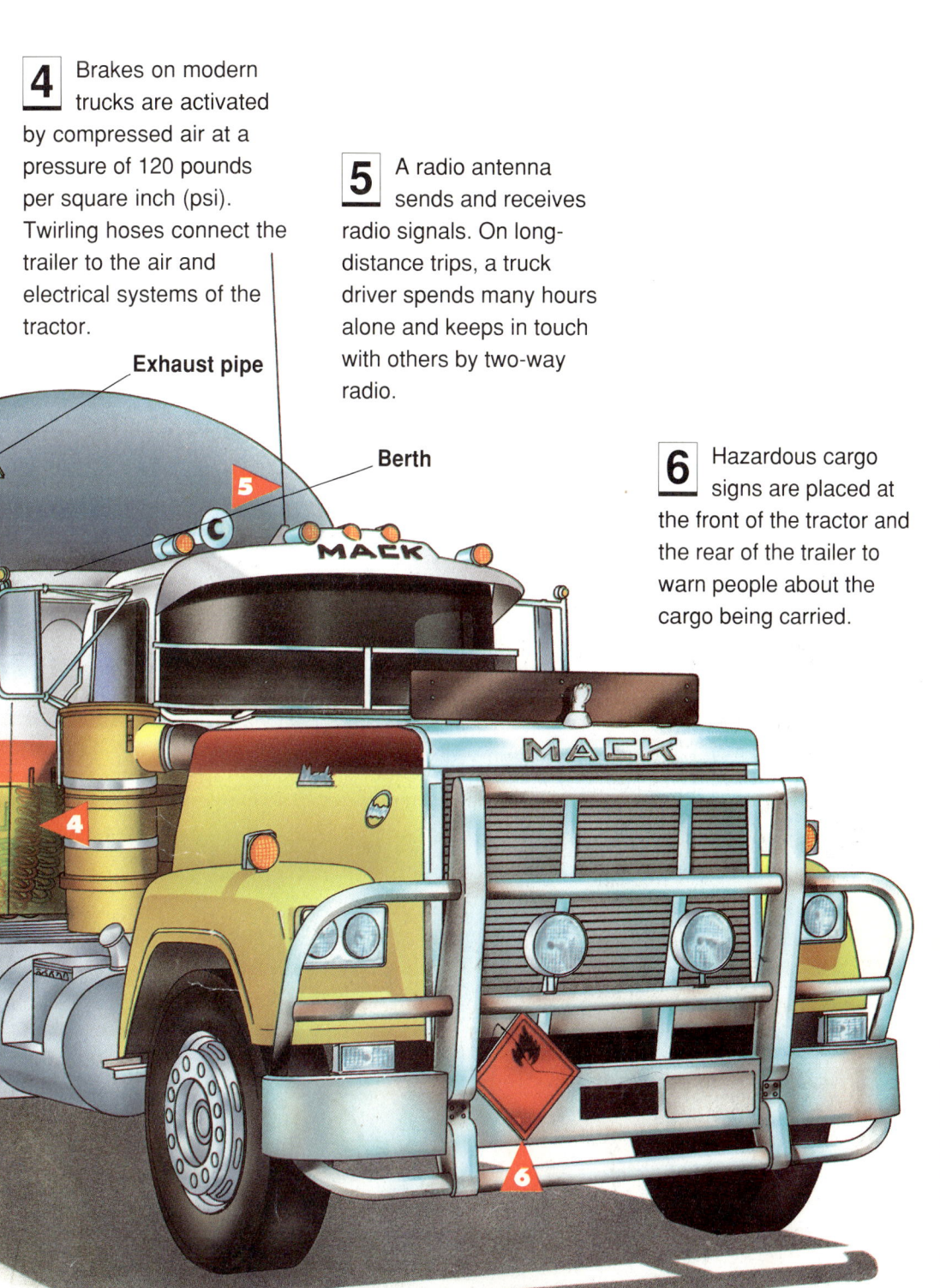

Exhaust pipe

Berth

Fuel tank

▶ Low Boy

Some trucking companies specialize in transporting very heavy or abnormal loads. Because of their extreme weight, a normal tractor-trailer cannot carry these loads. A very high-powered tractor and special low boy trailer have to be used.

The movement of heavy or abnormal loads is governed by law. Operators need a special license to drive this kind of truck. Sometimes a police car drives ahead of the truck to warn other drivers.

The truck being used to pull the low loader is a Scania 143.500 Topliner tractor. It is a 6x4 (six sets of wheels, four sets of them are drive wheels), which gives the tractor enough traction to handle the additional weight.

4 A revolving amber light and rear marker lights ensure that the low boy can be seen both day and night. The low boy travels very slowly, and cars might run into it.

Tractor

3 A sign on the truck warns others about the abnormal load. In Great Britain CAT 2 means that the total weight of the truck is no more than 176,000 pounds (80,000 kg), and its speed on the road is limited.

2 Big headlights are used on all trucks. A truck takes longer than a car to stop, so the driver must be able to see well ahead, especially at night. Scania is currently testing ultraviolet headlights.

1 The powerful Scania V8 500 hp engine has an electronic sensor which controls the amount of fuel injected into each of its eight cylinders.

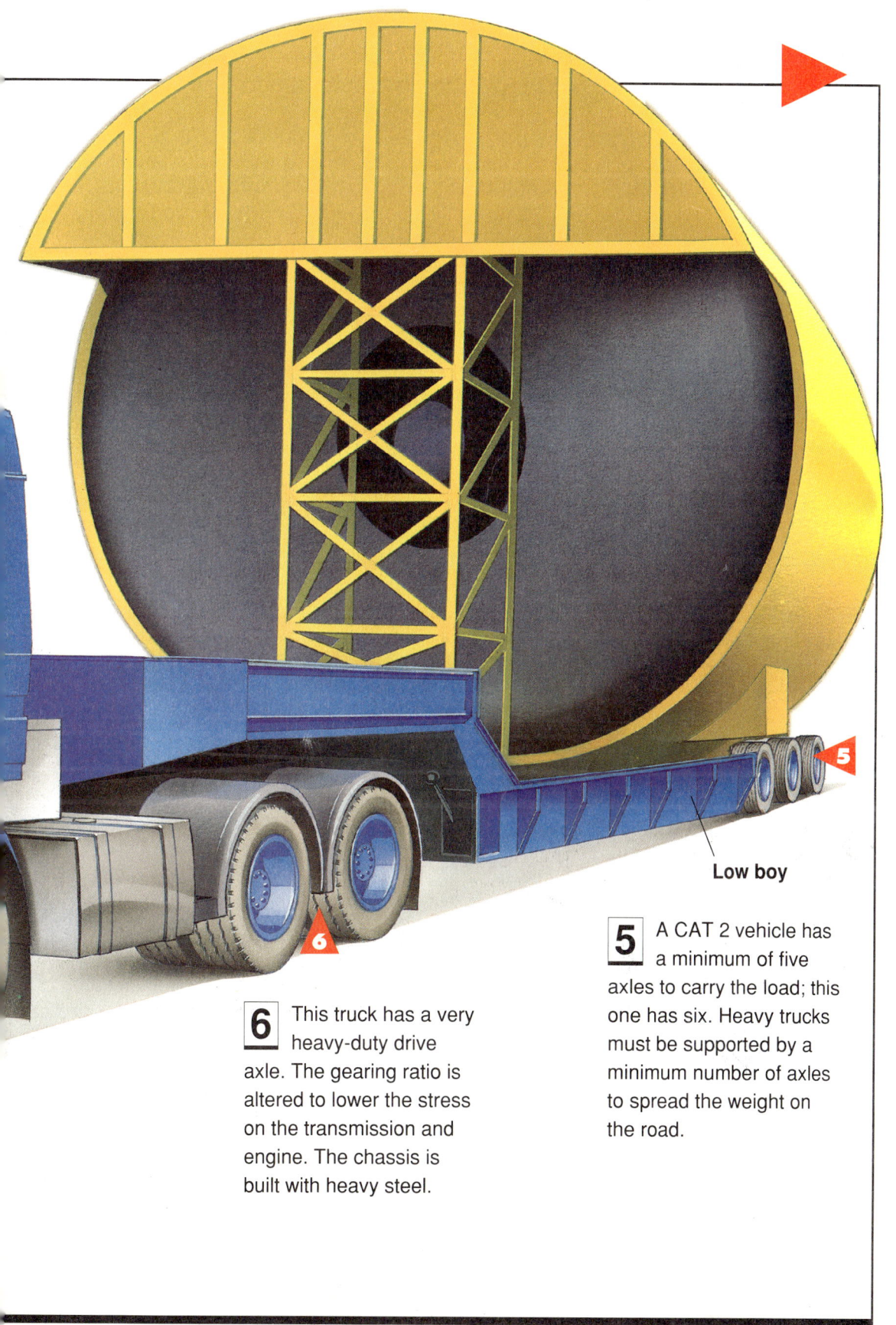

Low boy

6 This truck has a very heavy-duty drive axle. The gearing ratio is altered to lower the stress on the transmission and engine. The chassis is built with heavy steel.

5 A CAT 2 vehicle has a minimum of five axles to carry the load; this one has six. Heavy trucks must be supported by a minimum number of axles to spread the weight on the road.

Glossary

Aerodynamics
The study of how air affects the movement of objects

Articulated
Connected by joints. The joints allow the truck to corner and make it easier to maneuver.

Axle
A shaft or bar upon which the wheels revolve. Trucks have many axles and wheels to carry heavy loads.

Brake shoe
A curved metal cast that fits inside the brake drum at the axle. The shoe presses against the drum to slow the truck or car.

Chassis
The frame upon which the truck is built

Chock
A wedge-shaped piece of metal or wood placed behind a wheel to stop it from moving

Clearance
The distance from the ground to the lowest point of a truck

Cylinder
The place in the engine where fuel is ignited. The energy released forces the piston down inside the cylinder which drives a shaft.

Differential locks
A locking mechanism on the differential. The differential allows the wheels on an axle to turn at different speeds.

Drive axle
An axle connected by a drive shaft to the engine. The power of the engine is transferred to the wheels on the drive axle. These are called the drive wheels.

Fifth wheel
A coupling device; a turntable on the back of a tractor with jaws in which a kingpin from the trailer fits to link the two together

Gearing ratio
The relationship between the number of times the engine turns over and the number of times the wheels turn. A ratio of 1:1 means the drive wheels turn once for every engine revolution.

Gearshift
A gearstick connected to the transmission which allows gears to be changed

Gross vehicle weight
The total weight of the whole truck and its maximum load

Horsepower (hp)
The measurement of the power output of an engine

Hydraulic
Operated by movement of liquid. Power from a truck engine can be moved through liquid in a hose and used elsewhere, for instance to raise the body of a dump truck.

Hydraulic ram
The rod or piston in a cylinder filled with liquid in a hydraulic system. The ram transfers power from the engine.

Insulate
To prevent the movement of heat. Thick walls of insulation are built around a refrigerated trailer.

Psi
Pounds per square inch; a measure of air pressure

PTO
Power take-off; a device built into the transmission of some trucks to transfer some of the power of the engine away from the wheels to serve another purpose

Semitrailer
A type of trailer that has wheels only at the rear, the front end being supported by the tractor

Steering axle
An axle connected to the steering mechanism

Streamlined
Having a smooth shape so that air flows around easily

Suspension
A set of steel springs or air bags that helps cushion a vehicle from bumps in the road. Soft suspension systems help keep road damage to a minimum.

Synchromesh
System of gear changing in some truck transmissions. The gears are meshed together to make a smoother gear change.

Torque
The force of rotation of the engine. Where trucks are hauling very heavy loads in muddy conditions, the torque of the engine is more important than its power.

Traction
The act of pulling

Tractor
Truck used to pull semi-trailers or full trailers

Tread
The pattern of grooves in a tire

Turbocharger
A turbine driven by the engine's exhaust gases. It forces air into the engine under pressure, increasing its power.

Wheelbase
The distance between the center of the first axle and that of the rear one

31

Index

abnormal load 28
accident 22
aerodynamics 15, 19
air bags 14
air deflector 15
aluminum 10, 16
antiroll bar 22
antiroll cage 22
articulation point 19
automatic transmission 23, 25
axle 6, 8, 10, 11, 12, 14, 29

berth 13, 18, 27
body 6, 10, 12, 20
brake 18
   shoe 18

cab 6, 13
cab-over truck 16, 18, 22
car carrier 18-19
CAT 2 28, 29
chassis 6, 11, 29
chassis-cab 6
chock 21
chute 8
compressed air 27
computer 26
concrete 8
   mixer 8-9
construction industry 8, 20
conventional tractor 16-17, 26
crawler gear 7
crew cab 24
cylinder 7, 28

dangerous goods 26
diesel 20, 21, 22
diesel-electric drive system 20, 22
differential locks 9
door 25
drawbar truck 12-13
driver 18, 20, 21, 24, 26, 27
drum 8, 9
   brake 18
dump truck 20-21

electrical system 27
end dump 10-11
engine 7, 10, 24, 29
exhaust 9, 27

farm products 11
filter 21
Foden 4350 10-11
Freightliner FLD 112 16-17
fuel 15, 23
   injection 28

garbage truck 24-25
gross vehicle weight 6

headlight 22, 28
headroom 17
horn 11
horsepower (hp) 5, 7, 11, 20, 22, 28
hydraulic 7, 10, 19, 20, 22

insulation 14

ladder 13, 21
lights 28
low boy 28-29

mechanics 22
mirror 13, 21
Mk V 19

pallet 14
payload 10
Phoenix 15 24
power take-off (PTO) 10, 24

racing truck 22-23
radio 27
refrigerated truck 14-15
refrigeration unit 14
reverse gear 7, 13, 16
road 11, 14
rubber 20

Scania 143.500 Topliner 28-29
seats 17
semitrailer 14
shovel 11
side rail 12
side skirt 16, 23
sign, hazard 27, 28
sleeper compartment 13
speed 23
stability 8, 10, 12, 15, 19
steel 6, 10, 15, 19
steering 6, 10, 11
steps 18
straight truck 6–7, 8, 12, 24
streamlining 16, 23
suspension 14, 15

tanker 26-27
thermometer 14
tinted glass 17
tire 6, 20, 23
traction 20
trailer 12
transmission 6, 7, 16, 23
two-way radio 27

United States 16, 26

visibility 21
Volvo FS7 6-7

water tank 9
wheel 6
wheelbase 6, 24
windshield 21, 24

© 1994 Andromeda Oxford Limited

J 629.224 SAL
Salter, Andrew.

Trucks.

Raintree. c1995.

Glen Rock Public Library
315 Rock Road
Glen Rock, N.J. 07452

201-670-3970